Iggy Saunders: Monster Slayer
Written by Nic Mullen

D1280887

For D.M.
WITHOUT YOUR ENCOURAGEMENT AND SUPPORT THIS BOOK WOULD NOT HAVE BEEN POSSIBLE.
YOU HELPED TURN MY DREAM INTO REALITY.

There once lived a monster under Iggy Saunders' bed,
the kind of monster with claws and horns,
that filled sleepy children with dread.

He knew that it was there because he heard it every night. Tucked inside his covers, afraid to turn on the light.

It whispered his name, it tapped, and it taunted.

When Iggy closed his eyes it was his dreams that it haunted.

One night at bedtime, after his story was read, Iggy told his mother about the monster who lived under his bed.

First she made him look under the bed to see that nothing was wrong.

Then Iggy's mother said something that made him
feel strong.

"Iggy Saunders, monster slayer, you don't have
to fear. You're the hero of your story, and there
are no monsters here."

So Iggy Saunders went to bed, trying to be brave, knowing that when the monster came it was himself he'd have to save.

He crawled under his blankets and held his teddy tight.

His mother said, "GOODNIGHT LITTLE MONSTER-SLAYER,"

and then turned out the light.

Now Iggy laid in bed, staring at the moon. He braced himself, knowing the monster would come for him soon.

His eyelids got heavier with each passing second.
And Iggy could no longer resist sleep as it beckoned.

He awoke from a nightmare when his bed seemed to
rattle. Iggy focused on his breathing,
preparing for a battle.

First he heard the scratching, its claws running along the wall. Then Iggy saw the monster and it made his hair stand tall.

Prickly purple limbs hung ominously above him,
while curved horns sat where its eyes
should have been.

A twisted smile housed eyes that glowed green
It truly was the scariest thing Iggy had ever seen.

The monster was directly over Iggy, snarling as it
hovered. He felt it move away but kept
himself covered.

Quietly he counted, *ONE, TWO, THREE, FOUR, FIVE.*
He pinched his arm real hard to make sure he was alive.

Iggy took a deep breath and quickly hugged his teddy. Tonight was the night; he was finally ready.

He knew what he must do, to be the hero and save the day. For at the end of his bed there was a monster that he had to slay.

So Iggy pushed his covers down and stood bravely on his bed. Then suddenly he and the monster were standing head to head.

The monster opened up his jaws,

"There is no one here to save you,"

It said with a hissing sound.
But Iggy stood tall and brave, his courage finally found.

He looked that monster in the eyes and said to it so bravely,

"I am Iggy Saunders, monster slayer, and I am here to save me!"

For Iggy knew the secret to defeat the monster for good. Part of that secret was, he was the only one that could.

He screamed at the monster, looking straight in its eyes. When the words hit the monster you could hear its startled cries.

"YOU ARE NOT REAL!" THE BOY SCREAMED. THE MONSTER FELL BACKWARDS, SUDDENLY NOT AS SCARY AS IT SEEMED.

"YOU ARE NOT REAL!" Iggy shouted once

more. The monster reduced to a pile on the floor.

He yelled one more time, to ensure the job was done. Then Iggy Saunders, monster slayer, knew that he had won.

A heap of clothes now laid in front of him on the floor. An ugly purple sweater and a horned Viking hat from the Halloween before.

Iggy brushed the pile under his bed, even his baseball glove For he knew there was no longer anything to be afraid of.

So he climbed back up into his bed to sleep away the night.

Iggy slept straight through till morning because he had won the fight.

The End.

Made in United States
North Haven, CT
18 November 2021

11225008R00031